J. B. Moore

Homes for Thousands in the Beautiful Republican Valley,

Kansas

J. B. Moore

Homes for Thousands in the Beautiful Republican Valley, Kansas

ISBN/EAN: 9783337415259

Printed in Europe, USA, Canada, Australia, Japan

Cover: Foto ©Andreas Hilbeck / pixelio.de

More available books at **www.hansebooks.com**

HOMES

FOR THOUSANDS,

IN THE

BEAUTIFUL

REPUBLICAN VALLEY

OF KANSAS.

"EVERYBODY LIKES IT."

" Methinks I hear the onward tread
Of mighty nations yet to be,
The first low wash of wave
Where soon shall roll a human sea."

TOPEKA, KANSAS.
COMMONWEALTH PRINTING HOUSE.
1878.

THE REPUBLICAN VALLEY.

CLAY COUNTY, KANSAS.

Remarkable Progress in Material Development---The way they plant Civilization on the Old Buffalo Range---The wonderful Record of a Single De-
cade---A Sketch of Clay Center, one of the brightest towns in the Jay-
Hawker's Kingdom---Wakefield---And a Sketch of the English Colony---
Candid Review of a Splendid Country.

Our conceptions of the unseen are nearly always at fault.
We are apt to give too much play to fancy. The average
Yankee is as speculative in theory as he is intensely realistic
in practical things. His opinion of men and things he has
never seen is generally an exaggeration. He can draw on
imagination to a wonderful extent. But experience and sight-
seeing wear into his prejudices until, one by one, they are
dissipated and the naked truth is before him for appreciation.
Most persons go into a new country only to be disappointed.
They have exalted ideas of everything in the new land of their
hopes. It is their fair Utopia, and embodies every perfection
of climate, soil, production, topography and society. It is the
expression of their most extravagant hope and wish, the ob-
ject of their enthusiasm and excusable selfishness. They come
to the new country with high hopes and have not taken
into account the manifold hardships and drawbacks of pioneering. Realization dispels many a fair vision of the pioneer.
He drops down from his beautiful ideal world into the rough
practical ways of bread-getting and home-building. His land

of sunshine comes after all, to be like the rest of the world—
the theater of plodding, patient toil. If he be not a patient,
persistent worker, the new life on the border becomes a disappointment. He tires of the rough life and longs for the flesh
pots of his old native State. He has not the forecast to see
that the new country will become rich and prosperous, and
forgets that his fathers were pioneers in Ohio or Pennsylvania, and underwent a much harder and longer process of settlement and subjugation. He forgets too that all the prosperity of the old lands came of patient, persistent human labor.
He has yet to learn that experience is the best teacher man
ever had. What a vast army of these hopeful, over-sanguine,
visionary men have come to Kansas with an over-stock of bril-
liant hopes but with so little of the sterner virtues of patience
and endurance. It were impossible that they should fail of
disappointment, and it is easy to see that they will continue
to fail all the way through life. Thousands of these imprac-
tical, visionary men have come and gone, leaving these splendid savannas to be turned into gardens by more patient and
enduring men. They have done injury to the good name of
the State by their senseless complaining, but their opportunity
passed away with the "grasshoppers," the "drouth" and "hot
winds" of the early years.

Things are changed now. The days of doubt, trial and suf-
fering have passed, and there is not a more contented and
prosperous people in America than I find in the land of the
Jayhawkers. I have traveled over two-thirds of the State in
the most deliberate way; conversing with people of every
class and find more of the real spirit of contentment than in any
country I know west of the lakes and Alleghanies. For three
successive years they have grown immense crops of corn, wheat,
oats, barley and vegetables, and the herds of cattle, hogs, sheep,
horses and mules are altogether wonderful to see. There is no
real poverty anywhere, because there is no such thing as want.
The whole State is full of the comforts of life. Many of the
pioneers are without the higher luxuries of life because they
came but yesterday, with no capital but their naked hands,

and are just now breaking up the virgin prairie. But all around them are plenty of the common comforts, and they are within the reach of all. I should like to have my readers come with me to the Republican valley and see something of Kansas pioneering. Here is a valley 300 miles in extent, reaching from the bottoms of the Kansas away up to the Colorado hills, where its sources have an altitude of 3,000 feet above tide-water. For 250 miles of this distance it is settled by homesteaders who only eight, seven, six or four years ago fought off the Indians and buffalo from one of the fairest regions that ever gave welcome and a home to the pioneer. Now there are a dozen counties along this great valley, each with from 2,000 to 10,000 people. They are all engaged in production, and it would be hard to find in any country a finer exhibit of grain fields than one may find along this splendid water line. A dozen bright towns have sprung up, in half as many years, along the valley and every department of human life is represented by a multitude of hardy, successful workers. Clay Center, Concordia, Scandinavia, Superior, Red Cloud, Republican City, Wakefield and other towns are rapidly growing into prominence, and represent a country of almost incalculable resources.

Clay County may be taken as a fair representative of this valley region, and I take great pleasure in devoting the greater part of this pamphlet to its location, climate, soil, topography, agriculture, trade, schools, social life and future.

The location of the county is most desirable. It lies about eighty miles west of Topeka in the lower part of the Republican valley, and has an altitude of about 1,000 feet above the sea level. It is south of the Nebraska line about seventy miles. Of the settlement and organization of the county I give the following notes: As far back as 1855, a few families took claims in the south part of the county, well down towards the Kansas river. In 1857 and 1859 some excellent families settled in other portions of the county. In 1866 the county was formally organized, and to-day has a population bordering close upon 8,000. Up to 1865. the county was a wilderness, with here and there a settler. Herds of buffalo were grazing in the

Republican valley, and Indian forays were common. Indeed, the savages committed outrages down to a much later period. Since 1867 the settlement has been rapid. Save in the south half of the county, where the Kansas Pacific has a portion of its land grant, the whole county has been taken up and settled by homesteaders. The government has actually given away 300,000 acres to settlers from every part of the world in pre-emptions, homesteads and timber claims. Many of the early settlers abandoned their claims during the dry and grasshopper years, but their places were quickly taken by more courageous men, and there are few sections in the county to-day upon which some hardy pioneer is not working out "destiny." As to the people and their work I give the following notes: Illinois furnishes nearly twice as many as any other State. Next comes Iowa, and then the British Isles, followed by Missouri, Pennsylvania, Ohio, New York, Michigan, the Scandinavian States, Canada, Wisconsin, etc. The make-up of the population is excellent. It is much better than if it were constituted of a strictly homogeneous race, for it is broader, more cosmopolitan and generous than the provincial order that consists of the more local or clanish conditions. It is as safe to say that they have as high an average of intelligence here as in New York, Wisconsin or Iowa. It is a great mistake to suppose that the "*New West*" is peopled with a race of stupid, slow-going, thick-headed "numb-sculls." *That* class of people have neither the ambition or bravery to bring them out to the border. They stay at home, or soon go back East after finding themselves overshadowed by the thrift, energy and enterprise of their neighbors. There are as many bright, sharp, clear-headed, cultured people in Kansas as in any part of the country between the two oceans. For the most part they are the most ambitious people who come here. Their enterprise and taste and culture are expressed in the school system. As soon as two or more families are grouped in a neighborhood a school district is organized and the work of education is begun. Here in Clay county are ninety school districts, well organized with about seventy school houses, and yet the county is only about ten years old. There are other indications of good social order. There are upwards of about twenty church organizations in the county, and it is quite wonderful to see the social, mental and moral progress of the people, who only half a dozen years ago were on the border.

The face of the country is altogether charming. There are no swamps, no "sloughs," no marshes here. Along the water courses are valleys varying from forty rods to four miles in width. They are as fair as the fabled Eden, and cover fully twelve per cent. of the county. Beyond the valleys are the plateaus and high rolling prairies. Very little of Clay county is broken up so as to be unfit for cultivation. Not a hundred acres of the 522,300 acres in this beautiful county may be put down as waste land. Even the roughest and poorest would be a god-send to the Illinois or Ohio grazer. The soil is like most of Middle Kansas, a black vegetable mould, with a clay and limestone basis. No soil in the West is richer. It is from twenty inches to six feet deep, and the boy does not live in Clay county who will live to see it exhausted by continuous cultivation. The crops are splendid ; corn ranges from 40 to 80 bushels per acre, and it is safe to estimate the 40,000 acres of corn in the county this year at 2,000,000 bushels. There are about 35.000 acres of wheat, and the yield runs all the way from 16 to 40 bushels per acre. The wheat crop will probably aggregate 650,000 bushels. Oats, barley, rye, flax, sorghum, millet, and all the field and garden vegetables have a heavy growth. In fact, Clay county is blessed with generous crops and the question of the hour is "what shall we do with this produce ?" There are not half enough hogs and cattle in the county to consume the corn, while at least 200,000 bushels of old corn are still in the cribs.

Mixed farming is the order here. Nothing pays like it. The farmer has half a dozen strings to his bow. If one crop fails he has other resources to depend upon. A variety of small grains bring him cash in hand for August, September and October. In November and the winter months he has some well-fed hogs to turn off. Still later the cattle market on which he can place a few steers. It is far better than to rely on a single *special* crop. If that fails him the last resource is gone. I see for Clay county great and permanent prosperity with this great variety of agricultural resource. This versatility of production always brings wealth to the farming community.

The herd law has been a benefaction to this country. The poor homesteader could not have made headway with the indiscriminate cattle range. The law now compels the herding of live stock, and the grain grower has perfect immunity from damage to his crops. He has no need to fence, and here is a county with 8,000 souls, and a splendid agriculture, with no fences to mark the line between the farms. The protection afforded by the herd law is absolute. Of course large herds of cattle and sheep cannot be kept under such conditions, but population and production are twice as great as where there is no herd law.

Timber is found along the stream in sufficient quantity to supply all present needs, and almost every farmer is growing artificial forests. It only requires four or five years to grow an abundance of fuel, and these cultivated forests of cottonwood, walnut, maple, are coming to be the glory of the grand prairie landscapes. Cord wood is worth from $2 to $4 per cord, and will be cheaper five years from now. Of fine building stone there is no end. Magnesian limestone underlies the whole of Clay county. It is soft enough to saw, dress or plane into any desired shape, and makes the cheapest and most elegant building in the world.

The water courses are numerous and the water supply ample. It is not the dead, stagnant, insipid water of the lower lands, but clear, pure and bright as a mountain stream. The brook Republic flows from northwest to southeast through the heart of the county. Chapman's, Timber, Mulberry, Fancy, Deep and other creeks by the score give admirable water supply to every part of the county. The clear rock spring is not at all uncommon. Good wells are obtained at from fifteen to forty feet. They are growing fruits now in all parts of the county.

Half a dozen years ago, when the country was a lovely wilderness, the settlers thought Clay county would never become a fruit country. Now they are growing small fruits successfully with ordinary care. The superb orchards of Riley county (our next neighbor) have taught the Clay county people a wholesome lesson in fruit growing. Hundreds of young orchards and vineyards are coming into beauty and fruition. In a mild climate like this all the fruits of the latitude will flourish. The mild, dry winters, long genial summers, glorious Indian summer autumns, will give the same health and vigor to trees that they give to man and the lower animals. The fresh glow of health is on everything. The air has tone in it. There is neither malaria nor consumption here. Every living thing is in the normal condition. I could easily find 500 people in Clay county who have been cured of consumption and kindred diseases in this dry, bracing and equable climate.

It is remarkable to see how cheap lands are selling when one takes into account the advantages of the locality. We are not on the border here in Clay county. The border is 150 miles further out. It is a land of schools, churches, railroads and beautiful homes. A land of matchless valleys, covered with great luxuriant corn and wheat fields, and graced with lines of natural and artificial beauty. Towns and markets and newspapers are established here, and all human living is as well ordered as in Michigan, New York or New England. And yet lands are so cheap that one is really bewildered with the volume of essential wealth he may purchase with a little money. Wild lands may be purchased all the way from $1.75 up to $8 per acre, the latter price representing the fine bottoms of the Republican. Improved lands are selling at $3 to $15 and $20 per acre, the price always depending on the quality, location and improvement. Fine claims of 160 acres can be purchased at $350 to $500, with 30, 50 70 and 100 acres of plowed land, a fair house and other fixtures. The reason of this is the nearness to the border and the opportunities for settling government lands. It is the history of every new country. The original settlers, most of them, sell out for less than the cost of their improvements and push on the border. There are men all through this country who have followed up this process all the way from the Wabash valley westward. They are uneasy, restless men, who never stay long anywhere, and are always ready to sell. What splendid opportunities are here offering for men of modest means! A home and a farm for a few hundred dollars. And a large farm, too. A full *one hundred and sixty* acres. None of your cheap, drifting sand, nor your bleak, rocky mountain sides, in the region of everlasting frost and snow, but this dark, deep, rich alluvium, every acre of it rich enough for a market garden in the fairest climate; and God's own beautiful country. Who ever saw lovelier landscapes than these along the grand sweeping Republican up through Clay and Cloud counties? What a glorious realization of Western life may be seen in this fair and fertile region. It is easy to make a start here. A good yoke of cattle are worth $80 to $110; a span of common work horses, $100 to $175; a wagon just as cheap as in South Bend or Toledo; farm implements the same as in the Mississippi States, and everything else in the same ratio excepting pine lumber, which is fifteen per cent. higher than in the older States.

The sort of people wanted here are men who have some grit and will roll up their sleeves and go to raising potatoes, corn and hogs, prime wheat and pumpkins. The professions are pretty well filled now. There are plenty of merchants and about as many mechanics and common laborers as can find employment; but the world is hungry and wants bread and meat, and among the best places to grow them is Clay county, Kansas. There is room for just 15,000 more wide-awake, self-helpful working men, women and children in this county, and they can never find a better place to "stick their stakes."

But I must talk a little about the towns and people. Here in the geographical center of the county is Clay Center, its capital town. It has 1,000 souls and possibly 1,200. It is none of your sleepy, dead-alive towns, but a live, radiant, dashing city, with the heaviest mercantile trade of any town of its size and age in the Jayhawker State. They shipped 2,000 car

of grain from here last year, and will run up to 3,000
nough this year.   Here is the upper end of the Junction
& Fort Kearney Railroad, and it commands the products
e Republican valley for sixty or eighty miles.   I have no
, about the shipment of 800 car loads of cattle and hogs
from this point the coming year.   The town is in the full tide
of the grain trade now, and the business streets are a perfect
jam from morning to night.   Hundreds of grain wagons jog
along down the valley from Cloud, Jewell, Republic, Mitchell,
Smith and other counties in the splendid upper country.   Whole
trains of teams come here with corn, wheat, rye, barley, sweet
potatoes and fat hogs, and carry back lumber and all kinds of
merchandise.   It is just such a sight here in the business hours
(and they last from daylight till midnight) as some of the
sleepy, conservative, provincial merchants of the "down East"
country. who believe that Kansas is a pandimonium of grasshoppers, Comanches. border ruffians and horse thieves, should
come and see.   I can show them half a hundred such towns,
at this season, in this great State, but Clay Center answers
my purpose exactly in this case.   It is refreshing and reassur-
ing to look into the grain elevators, stores, shops, banks and
land offices and see the busy life they live in this young and
expanding city.   It is only six or seven years since the town
site was a wild prairie—now it is one of the liveliest little cities
this side of 'Frisco and the Golden Gate.   They have half a
dozen grain warehouses, a splendid steam flouring mill, two
banks. a dozen stores. as many more offices, a fine school house,
several churches and one of the best newspapers in the State.
The city gets inspiration from the magnificence around it, and
from the sterling character of its business men.   It takes men
to make a city, and here they are ; prime, strong, self-reliant
men, who move about as if there was some warm Western
blood in them, and as if they were born to business.   Most
of them started with little means, and some of them with only
their ambition and empty hands.   To-day they are carrying
great stocks. or handling a heavy business, and they seem to
do as if it were the first, middle and last work of life.   They

are the sort of men to build a city, and to such as they the work becomes easy in a country of great native resources like this. A dull, stupid, thick-headed man could not live in such an atmosphere as this. It is too hot and too fast for him. Life means something, and Clay Center is no place for dreamers.

The Quaker City Mills are the prime attraction of Clay Center. Next to the railroad they are the best local stimulus to general trade. They are 35x78 feet, four stories high, have four run of buhrs, and are named in honor of the Quaker City Machine Works, of Indianapolis, which furnished them throughout with a splendid equipment of the latest and most approved mill machinery. They are supplied with the best middlings purifiers for making the patent flour, and turn out 120 barrels daily of the best flour made in Kansas.

It takes two banks to transact our business, two mills to grind our flour and feed. We have a fine water power already improved to give impulse to Clay Center and it is full of large hearted hospitable, enterprising men who are putting their impress upon the social and material life around them. They have built a bright and prosperous city in four years. There was really little here before the railway came in '73. This city is the creature of a well managed railroad corporation and a group of live, earnest business men. What its future may be as the road is extended further up the valley remains to be seen, but with such a company of men to foster a town and such a country as Clay county to sustain it there can be no question about a future city here of 4,000 to 5,000 souls. A dozen miles down the railway and valley is Wakefield, a pretty village on the west side of the Republican, settled by a colony of Englishmen under the lead of Rev. Richard Wake and named in his honor. Mr. Wake and his friends came here and founded the colony in 1869. There are about three hundred English families in the colony and they are generally doing well. They are people of excellent character and could not have chosen a finer region for colinization. The village has a lovely location on a southeasterly slope overlooking the river valley and railway. The valley is full two miles wide here and the river is fringed with a stately border of cottonwoods. Beyond, on the "eastern shore" are the grand bluffs and back of them the fine table lands reaching half a dozen miles away to the pretty Welsh village and colony of Bala. At the foot of the village on the south is the pretty winding tree-shaded Sylvan creek and a little to the north the bold headlands of Cedar Bluff. The great valley of the Republican is in view for miles as it drifts southward to the broad Kansas bottoms. What a beautiful land is this for the new heritage of our English cousins.

It is interesting to know what they have in this beautiful region and village. They have a soil of inexhaustible fertility, a splendid corn crop, yielding from forty to ninety bushels to the acre, wheat fields that run from fifteen to thirty-five bushels, and royal crops of oats, barley, rye and vegetables. They have a country abounding in landscapes as fair as the vale of Cashmere. Grand prairie reaches and beautiful groves; clear fountains, brooks and ravines. A land of sunshine and abounding health. In the village they have a fine stone school house, a good school and hundreds of pretty building places for the new settlers' cottage. They have, too, building stone fit for a palace.

What they want is a good mill, on the water power that is going to waste in full sight of the town, on the Republican. This is a fine water power, and the builder of a mill here will find a rock bottom for his dam with free use of power and a country good enough to furnish all the patronage he wants. They want some herds of cattle and droves of hogs to feed upon the immense and cheap corn crop. Above all they want hundreds of good, resolute workingmen to buy and cultivate these fertile lands and make homes in a fair and inviting land. Let it not be forgotten that Wakefield is a railroad town and offers good openings to good men from every clime.

MARKETS.

This is a matter of interest to all the people of Kansas, Nebraska, Minnesota. Wisconsin, Missouri, Iowa, and other States west of the Mississippi and east of the Rocky Mountains. It is a matter of interest and speculation to the capitalist of the East. It is a matter of great importance to the person coming from the East to the more extreme Western States, and it is especially of interest to the men coming West who intend engaging in agriculture. The question of markets has kept many persons from leaving the high-priced and worn-out lands of the Eastern and old settled States from coming to the productive lands of the West. The story of "too far to market" has influenced many a good, industrious and honest renter of high-priced lands in other States (when the year's crops would barely pay the rent) from packing his goods, and with his hard-working wife and family, coming to this beautiful valley and getting him a cheap farm of his own, where every hours' work pays twenty per cent. interest.

Now, for the interest of all concerned, let us look to this matter of markets a little. New York, of course, is too far for the people of Kansas to think of sending corn in the grain, and as a rule wheat will not pay to send to New York in the grain ; but cattle or stock of any kind will pay to ship as well from the State of Kansas as from the States of Illinois. Indiana or Ohio. The freight on a car load may be more than from those States, but the cost of raising in this State is not so much by one-fourth as in those States and all other Eastern States. The winters being so much shorter it takes less feed, and the feed being on the ground without expense to the farmer to raise it by planting, makes it much cheaper ; and less grain feeding, on account of the abundance of summer feed, makes the expense of raising the stock one-fourth or a third less than in the States named. This enables the stock raiser to make as much or more from his shipments than the Illinois farmer. It is certainly well understood by my farmer friends of the East, where they have to feed six months for a regular winter as it comes, that their stock kept on dry feed that length of time will not turn out in spring in as good flesh or as large growth as they will when kept only three months on the same kind of feed. Add this to the difference in the amount of feed, the difference in the cost of the feed, and the expense of help in feeding that stock through three months more of winter than here, and the cost will overbalance the expense for freight from here to those States.

Now, as to the wheat of our State, which forms a very important part of our farm products as well as wealth to the farmer—what will you do with that? We say, upon looking at the States west of the Mississippi and east of the Rocky Mountains, it seems to have been only in the wisdom of the Creator that one portion of the country should be to the other a positive necessity to bring about that which is now so rapidly taking place—the settlement of all this vast territory by the people from all points of the compass. All the eastern (as well as the western) slope of the mountains from the isthmus to the British Possessions is a mining country, and but little else ; and west of us, and no further from us than New York is from the States I have named, are the great mining countries of Colorado, Northern Mexico, Arizona, Montana and others that are filling up with people, cities are growing as by magic in the valleys, the hills and mountains of those countries are becoming spotted with the tent and the shanty of the miner. The most wonderful coal, iron and silver mines of the world are being opened out and brought into use by the energy and industry of the American nation, and millions of consumers are wending their way to those fields of wealth and must be fed. This, as our standpoint, we see the overruling hand of Providence in making the great States of Kansas, Nebraska, Minnesota, Iowa and Missouri agricultural and farming countries, to raise the necessary products to feed the swarming miners that are tunneling the mountains. Railroad companies are striving with each other, and stretching out their lines to these immense beds of ore for the purpose of freighting the living masses to their fields of labor, and the food to feed them, while they crush them to pieces and smelt them into bars of iron, bricks of silver and nuggets of gold; and again return loaded down with the coal and iron of those mountains, for the benefit and use of the producer of these beautiful valleys, rich with the growth of its fertile soil. But this is not our only place to look to for a grain market. The city of St. Louis, with its outlet to the gulf, is becoming a very good market. Again, Galveston on the gulf will soon be a New York to the West for all foreign markets. With all of these around us it is, we believe, only a matter of a few years until the West will be better situated for good foreign, as well as home markets, than the States of Illinois, Indiana, Michigan or Ohio.

With our short winters, productive soil and a country every acre of which can be brought into cultivation with very little expense, is it to be wondered at that these prairies are fast filling up?

BIG WEALTH.

The following statement, furnished us by the accommodating officials of the Kansas Pacific Railroad in this city, speaks volumes for the business of Clay Center and the great Republican valley:

Shipments in car load lots of grain, stock, &c., from Clay Center during October, 1877

Wheat	86
Rye	50
Barley	30
Chop	26
Broomcorn	6
Corn	18
Oats	1
Castor beans	1
Lumber	1
Flour	2
Hogs (416 head)	8
Cattle (49 head)	3

Recapitulation.—Grain, 212 cars; flour, 2; broomcorn, 6; lumber, 1; stock, 11; total, 232 cars.—*Clay County Dispatch.*

WATER. .

One of the chief advantages which the Republican valley has over other western counties is her vast and inexhaustible water resources. Water is procured anywhere in this valley at a trifling expense, and at a depth of from five to twenty-five feet, owing generally to the distance from and the height above the bed of the Republican river.

The water is clear as crystal, and very cold; it is obtained by drive wells, to which pumps are attached.

The vast body of water underlying this entire valley furnishes a sub-irrigation, and the soil, when once broken, remains damp and mellow the year round, no matter how dry the season.

OUR RAILROAD FACILITIES.

The Junction City & Fort Kearney Railroad, leading in a northwest direction up the Republican valley from Junction City on the Kansas Pacific Railroad to Fort Kearney on the Union Pacific in Nebraska, has had its terminus during the past four years at Clay Center, giving this place a wonderful impetus, and very materially enhancing the value of her property and the surrounding country. This road gives us an outlet both east and west, Clay Center being only about thirty miles from the Kansas Pacific road. It is, however, now being extended (the track is to-day being rapidly placed upon the road-bed) some fifteen miles up the valley to Clifton, where it forms a junction with the *Central Branch*. The Kansas Central (narrow gauge) running from Atchison, Kansas, due west, and now completed to within a few miles east of Clay Center, is also being rapidly extended, and will form a junction with the Junction City railroad at Clay Center the coming summer.

There are also other roads being projected. One from Beatrice, Neb., running south via Clay Center. Also, one from a point on the Central Branch via Clay Center and Great Bend on the Santa Fe railroad. No section was ever better situated

2

to receive the *full benefits* from all the diverging lines which
must tap it from every direction. No community ever need
desire better railroad facilities. All these roads are competing
lines to and from *rival cities*, which must have the effect of
reducing freights. It is thought, too, in the very near future,
a road will be built from some of the main points on the
Union Pacific, giving us an air line to Galveston, Texas, the
natural shipping point for a large portion of this country.

KANSAS THE BEST WHEAT-GROWING STATE IN THE UNION.

[From the Valley Banner.]

ABILENE, DICKINSON CO., KAN.

Land Commissioner Kansas Pacific Railroad:

DEAR SIR: Your favor, asking from me a statement of the
general result of my wheat crop and the wheat crop of this
vicinity, is received.

As you are aware, I do not reside on my farm, neither do I
claim to be a farmer in the ordinary sense of the word. I
make wheat raising a specialty on my farm. Every operation
connected therewith, from the time the prairie is first broken
until the grain is marketed, is done wholly by contract; those
employed furnishing themselves in every particular.

The method of operation is as follows: The prairie is broken
during the months of May and June, but may be prolonged
till the middle of July. By the 20th of August the soil is
once thoroughly harrowed over, it being wholly unnecessary
to replow the ground. Then seed, at the rate of one bushel
to the acre, is scattered broadcast, and the seeding is completed by two more harrowings, making a total cost so far, including the seed, of $5 per acre. By the 20th of June follow-
ing, the grain is ready for harvesting, which can be hired done
with headers at the rate of $2 per acre, including stacking.
Threshing costs eight cents per bushel, and the cost of mar-
keting depends of course upon the distance hauled. If the
grain yields twenty bushels to the acre, which is a low average,

and the distance from town not more than three miles, the total cost—$4 more being added to the cost of seeding—aggregate $9 per acre. The wheat averages rather above $1 per bushel, so that the clear profit of $11 dollars per acre remains, and everything hired done.

The straw, to a farmer, is worth $2 per acre for stock feed.

A second crop can be grown at an outlay of not more than fifty cents per acre, aside from seed and the mere cost of drilling the grain into the ground, without the necessity of re-plowing—taking the precaution to clear the land of all litter by burning off its stubble. The ground is so fertile that even three crops of wheat may be grown in succession on one plowing, and that for the first one. Two years ago I put in 500 acres, pursuing the foregoing method. My yield was nineteen bushels to the acre, and it sold at ninety cents per bushel, wheat in 1874 having borne a lower price than was ever known here before; it afterwards during the following winter advanced to $1.15 per bushel. I have just finished threshing 26,800 bushels as the yield of 1,200 acres, an entire average of 22¼ bushels to the acre, which I have sold at $1.05¼ per bushel, making a total net profit of $18,974. My straw is worth fully $1,500 more, and the land is increased at least $5 per acre from being placed under cultivation. By this you will see the results of my own experience are decidedly satisfactory, and as to the others around, as I wrote you some weeks ago, I have never seen things look more hopeful than now. The acreage of winter wheat is nearly double that of any previous year, and twenty-five per cent. better, and the same may be said of nearly all other crops; the result of all of which is, that a general spirit of satisfaction and contentment prevails, and many a home will have cause to bless the grasshopper year for having instilled a lesson of economy and determined industry.   Respectfully.   T. C. HENRY.

FACTS.

Twelve good reasons why you should come to Clay County.

1. Because it is always healthy.

2. Because it is well watered.

3. Because it has a rich soil and fine farming lands.

4. Because it has short mild winters.

5. Because it only requires moderate means to start here.

6. Because it has good schools, churches and all the advantages of old settled communities.

7. Because real estate is rapidly increasing in value.

8. *Because it will pay.*

9. Because you can get a good improved farm for less than what it would cost you to put these same improvements on a homestead.

10. Because it is a good wheat, corn and stock country.

11. Because, from our mild climate and the natural peculiarities of our soil, it is destined to become the finest fruit section in the West.

12. Because all the above advantages, with many others not mentioned, which are actually and absolutely true, go to make up a country altogether desirable, in which any person with industry and judicious management can not only make a good living but secure for them and their children, should they be so fortunate as to have any, a beautiful home and a competence for old age. The Republican valley, for its *natural scenery* peculiar to this country, is one of the most beautiful valleys ever viewed by the admiring eye of any lover of natural scenery. It has been our good fortune to view the finer portions of many of the States of our Union, and we hardly know where to look for another section of country which would present so many *natural advantages* and so few objections. Everything seems to have been prearranged to meet the wants and conveniencies of its settlers. The position which Clay county occupies is such that it must *ultimately be gridironed with railroads,* so that it matters very little in what part a man may settle, he will not long be more than four or five miles from some main or branch line. Already the roads are laying down their iron, and but a short time will elapse ere we shall have three or four roads instead of what we now have running into Clay Center. All of these things should be taken into consideration in selecting a point to locate. The county is well settled, every desirable claim being occupied and more or less improved. The pioneer hardships are passed, and the county is fast gaining the appearance and advantages of an old settled country, having already made wonderful strides in every branch of industry leading to wealth and refined civilization. We

have mills, stores, markets, railroads, school houses, churches and well organized society. *Many of the settlers*, though having come with nothing, have by hard work and perseverance made considerable improvements, but are of course in cramped circumstances and willing to sell their claims, and with the means thus obtained push on further west and commence again; others are not satisfied to live in a civilized country, and when they find civilization crowding upon them, they sell if they can and move on to the frontier. So it goes. And still others, of a restless and discontented, roving disposition, who never know when they are well off, embracing their first opportunity to sell, priding themselves on the fact that they would sell anything a man would buy of them, even to the clothes they wore. The lands and farms of all these classes are fast changing into the hands of more capable, energetic men, who have the means to improve the advantages thus gained. Kansas will open its great welcome arms to receive *a larger immigration* this winter and coming spring than ever settled in any State in a single season, so great has been our success and so well and so far spread the information. Clay and adjoining counties must receive much the larger portion, occupying the position and offering the advantages they do. All these lands are being bought by men of means, who are buying them for their future homes. There can be *but one result*—the rapid increase in the value of land. The *great advantage gained* by the purchaser of these lands is that he practically *homesteads* in a settled country, and gets the land already improved for about what it would cost him to put on the improvements. In other words, he may purchase the right to *homestead* a particular piece of land *already improved*, thereby saving himself the labor of improving, and yet be able to commence farming immediately, having at the same time all the advantages of the homesteader: the protection of our exemption laws and the exemption from taxation for several years.

AN IMPORTANT QUESTION.

How can I free myself from this burden of debt and better my condition? Thousands of men all over the Eastern and Middle States are asking themselves this question every day. Who can answer it? We say, sell your farm or property which is encumbered, possibly past redemption, and with the surplus, though it may be small, purchase a farm in the Republican valley, and with less encumbrance and longer time for payment, prepare yourself for what is before you. In making the change you get into a beautiful country and a delightful climate, and one of the best agricultural sections in the United States. The soil is rich and strong, the land new and productive, and everything is in your favor. You have access to Eastern and Western markets over competing lines, which give just as reasonable rates of freight as any routes in the East. Our system of railroad transportation (see page 17) rivals any section in the West. And even our present low prices, notwithstanding our "*great distance from market*," are paying our people twenty per cent. *more profit* on their labor and investment than Eastern farmers can realize on theirs, with all their so called advantages, so far superior are our facilities for producing grain, stock and all kinds of produce. The old objection, "too far from market," has been wiped out, and to-day we have better markets for our productions than the Middle States.

OUR CROPS.

For three successive years Clay county has had three successful crops. And the prospect now before us promises fairer than ever before. Owing to the success of the wheat crop the past season we have now a larger acreage on ground than any previous year, which owing to the frequent rains this fall is in the very finest condition possible. The fields and valleys as far as the eye can reach are beautiful with a rich and luxuriant growth of wheat and rye. We find, notwithstanding the large amounts shipped and fed, a considerable quantity of old corn yet on hand, for which holders could have realized 35 to 40 cents per bushel, delivered here in Clay Center, at different times during the past summer. There is in addition to this a very large crop (in some instances averaging 80 bushels to the acre) now being cribbed from our fields, from which it is not unreasonable to expect that we may realize at least as much the coming summer. For our wheat the past season our farmers realized from 85 cents to $1 per bushel for what they have sold, and the prospect now is that they will realize even a better price for what they have on hand. While the average yield in all our crops has been large and very satisfactory to the producer, we are far from supplying the demand, so great is the demand of our Western market for all kinds of produce. Never were such opportunities thrust upon the producer before. His productions are literally "gobbled" and hurled to the mining districts, from whence comes the ever increasing demand for meal, flour, butter, cheese, eggs, poultry and cured meats. Especially does this last *production* open a remunerative field for those disposed to avail themselves of its profits. The cost of producing corn is comparatively small, and by feeding it out to hogs our farmers can realize something over 40 cents per bushel, even when he places his hogs on the market at our lowest price. If he chose to butcher and cure the meat instead, it will net him an average increased profit of 50 per cent. over and and above the profit obtained by selling them alive, or a fraction less than 62 cents per bushel for all the corn fed—a very handsome profit (as any one can see) for his extra labor and trouble of curing his meat before offering it for consumption.

These are not by any means the only sources of remunerative farming. Indeed, mixed farming is the order here. Corn, wheat, rye, oats, barley, potatoes and all the other products for consumption are raised with equal facility, trifling expense and one-half the labor required in the older States. Closely connected with our grain and produce comes our *stock*, for raising which our facilities surpass every other section, and are bound to place us in advance of every stock-growing region in the West. Our fine grazing lands, our beautiful creeks and streams, always giving an abundant supply of pure running water, and the easy access to never-failing water even in the absence of these, gives us a natural advantage over other sections that may have the lands but not the water, which is bound to place our valley in the lead in this as in other respects, and make our farmers and stock raisers the stock kings of the West.

OUR WATER POWER.

The Republican River Awaiting Development for Mills and Manufactories.

Clay county, it is safe to say, offers better sites for mills and manufactories along the banks of the Republican river than can be found elsewhere. We only have room to mention two or three points where water power could be developed by an outlay of capital, small in comparison to the value of the power gained.

Already a dam has been placed in the river at Clay Center and the power utilized by a good flouring mill, now running night and day. But a few hundreds of dollars expended in raising the dam at this point would furnish power for several mills and manufactories instead of one. The raceway is a natural one, and so situated that by properly placing the mills or manufactories along the banks an unlimited amount of power might be obtained at this point.

There are two other points—Wakefield, some nine or ten miles down the river, and Morgantown, some eight or nine miles up the river. Both locations are in themselves excellent, not to be surpassed, and both towns are really in need of a mill to give them a new impetus and supply the wants of the surrounding country. Such openings *are not* found every day, where there is the want and necessity of the power, and also the power right at hand awaiting capital and enterprise to develope that power and supply a want felt all through the county. Any one investigating this matter will find it exactly as represented, only the real facts and advantages in the case are better than they are here written. Nothing less than *a fortune awaits* the lucky individual or individuals who may first seize these opportunities and turn them to their account.

A mill at one point on this river nets its owner a clear profit of $1 per hour for twenty-four hours a day, week in and week out. The Quaker City steam mills at this place, Clay Center, have during the year past shipped to Denver alone, that being only one of their several shipping points, a car load of chop per day on an average the year through, and this too in addition to their large custom and merchant work with which they are constantly crowded. I only drop in this to illustrate the fact that there are openings here in this business which it will pay men with capital to investigate, and to show that there is a paying demand for our flour and

feed and a supply of grain and produce from our fields that will
warrant the development of the power at hand. Just above Clay
Center some three or four miles, at a point known as Rock Ford,
is an opening and a power than which no better can be found the
world over. The bank on the west side of the river rises from 20
to 100 feet in height, and on the other of such height that it would
be impossible that it could ever overflow or burst through. The
bed of the river is *solid rock* from one side to the other, giving the
finest foundation for a dam that nature could form. It has been
passed upon by those who are judges of water powers, and their
judgment is that no better could be found. Nature even could
not have made a better one had she made one to order. Right at
hand are rock enough to build the dam and plenty to spare, and
everything seems to invite energy and enterprise to develop these
sources of power. The power can be bought for a reasonable sum,
including forty acres of fine land that goes with it, and all lays not
a mile from the railroad. The few points mentioned are not by
any means the only ones at hand, but enough to show that we have
them here. What we want is men, good, live, enterprising men, to
open up and utilize these sources of wealth.

WHY YOU SHOULD COME TO KANSAS.

In almost every town, city and county throughout the Eastern,
Middle and Western States, there are those who are almost per-
suaded to "go to Kansas." They read the wonderful stories of our
productive soil, our splendid climate, and the rapid progress made
in the development of our apparently inexhaustible natural resources, and while inclined to doubt, or regarding these glowing
accounts as eminations from the fertile brain of land agents or
speculators, the stubborn statistics come along with their convincing proofs, and the hitherto incredulous are forced to admit that
ours is a wonderful country. Then viewing the situation again,
another standpoint is presented. They argue that by dint of hard
labor and frugal management a living is assured in the East or
North, and by removing to the new west, aside from undergoing
the inconveniences peculiar to a new country, the grasshoppers
may devastate the land. They remember the wail that went up
from Kansas sufferers a few years ago. And then the "Great
American Desert" is certainly liable to suffer from extreme
drouth. Logical conclusions, apparently, for those whose lights
are hidden under a bushel, but not in accordance with the facts.

Kansas and Kansans have indeed suffered as have no other peo-
in this great nation. First, through the terrible border war, with
the national struggle following in its wake, attended by a drouth,
then followed the locusts and corrupt politicians. But the Rubi-
con has been crossed. Kansas has survived all these calamities.
When these evils came upon her she was in her infancy and help-
less. To-day she stands forth in her own strength, able to do bat-
tle against these visitations combined, and then assist to feed the
millions beyond her border. While we feel secure, and peace has
shed her broad pinions o'er all the land, yet we have as much reason
to anticipate another border war as a visitation from the herbage-
devouring grasshopper. They have had their day in this country, as
they had a hundred years ago in New England, or two thousand years
ago in Egypt. They have fulfilled their mission and gone hence. As
regards our country being subject to drouth, it is no more liable to

suffer from that cause than any other State—else the science of meteorology (and it is a science in these days of "old Probs.") is false in theory, and all the experiments of the years that are passed go for naught. These convincing truths are presented each year, that as the country is brought under a state of cultivation, as the soil is changed and timber grown, the humidity of the atmosphere changes and the rainfall increases. We are not so irreverent as to assume that man in his weakness is controlling these matters especially, here in Kansas, but rather that natural causes are working these changes for us, so that he who runs cannot help noting them. A wise Providence never designed these broad prairies and grand valleys, having a rich soil three or four feet in depth, to remain a wild waste and uncultivated wilderness. These are choice grounds, the dooryard and garden of a great nation; and the steady tread of coming feet is now heard within the gate upon the waving lawn of "Uncle Sam's" homestead. Then to return to our "Why." You should come to Kansas, for you can in a brief period secure a home. Our rich lands are cheap and within your reach. You should come from the hills of New England, from Michigan, Wisconsin, Minnesota and Iowa because you with your stock will not be housed up from five to seven months each year by the snows and cold north blasts. Our climate is pleasant and extremes are not great. You should come where your labor, now wasted on the sterile hills and among stones and stumps is so poorly rewarded. With less labor you can fill large granaries and gaze on your own herds. You should come to the new Southwest because it is the most healthy portion of our country. You should come because by coming you will better your condition financially as well as physically. You should come and come soon, because other thousands are coming. You should come and share with us the proud distinction of having assisted in building up the Kansas of the future.

LANDS AND LOANS

In this department I lead the county and region surrounding (Pardon if I take a little honest pride in the fact.) My real estate department embraces 40,000 acres of lands from the stock range at $1.50 per acre to the medium lands at $3 and $4. The valley lands at $5 to $8. The partially improved claim of 160 acres at $2 to $4, and the well improved farm at $6 to $15 and $20 per acre owing to their location and distance from market. I have lands in every part of this and neighboring counties to sell on almost any terms desired. I have also city and town lots and dwellings in Clay Center and other towns in our valley. Never before were such opportunities and inducements offered to those coming West. Never before was there such an opportune time for coming.

The difficulties and inconveniencies attending the settlement in a new country have all been surmounted—the rough pioneer work has all been done and many of the early settlers have already sold out and gone further west and the *fruit* and benefits of their toil and labor, the *profits of their investments* are awaiting those who come to till their places.

Several instances came under my observation where parties from the East purchased farms, and the first season following (this season) raised enough wheat on the farm to pay every dollar of the purchase money, and all the expenses of raising besides. Of course these are exceptions, nevertheless they are facts, and it can be done by the industrious careful man.

We get as good a price for our wheat and a better for our corn, hogs and other produce in comparison to the cost of production than any producer in Indiana, Illinois and many of the Eastern States. This is not merely an assertion but an actual fact (as any one can learn by investigation) even counting our produce at the lowest *average* price that may be realized.

What is it that "makes your living" and pays a man's debts if it is not the surplus which accumulates over and above the cost of production. When you come to "strike a balance" and compare notes you will find a large balance *in favor* of the West and the Western producer. Not only this, but every one can see that at the present rate of immigration and the increasing demand for our lands and property, lands cannot long remain at their present price. Indeed, the bottom has been reached, and already we feel the reaction in prices which are growing firmer every day. The natural result of this works to the advantage of those investing here. Property can no longer depreciate but must rapidly increase in value so that those who invest must shortly double on their investment. There is indeed a vast difference between investing here and investing where values have been inflated and are now fast depreciating. The Republican Valley is in the Golden Belt and destined to be the richest agricultural district in the world.

OPPORTUNITIES.

We drop in below a few descriptions of a few of the farms and lots we have to sell. Besides these we have numberless others to sell which we have no room to place here. What we want is to have you tell us about what you want and we will write you what it will cost and on what terms it can be had. Awaiting your orders and inquiries, we respectfully submit the following farms and lots for sale. For further information, address J. B. MOORE, Clay Center, Clay county, Kansas.

No. 1.—160 acres, 6 miles from Clay Center; 30 acres under cultivation; house 14x18, stable, well and other improvements. Price, $1,500, time on part.

No. 2.—Splendid farm 9 miles from Clay Center, containing 160 acres, 115 acres under cultivation; house 16x20, three rooms, good cellar. 1,000 fruit trees; 80 rods hedge; shade trees around whole farm; 8,000 trees in nursery; one acre strawberries, etc. Price $20 per acre.

No. 3.—160 acres —— miles from Clay Center; 30 acres under cultivation; house 16x18.

No. 4.—160 acres —— miles from Clay Center; 30 acres under cultivation; house 16x18 with basement kitchen, stable, etc.; 100 fruit trees, grape vines, etc.; 3,000 forest trees. Price, $1,500.

No. 5.—One of the best improved farms in the county; 160 acres, 40 acres under cultivation, 40 acres fenced for pasture; one mile forest trees 5 to 6 years old; 500 peach trees, 100 apple trees and about 100 cherry, plumb, etc.; orchard surrounded with forest trees; house 20x24, 1½ story, 3 rooms, good cellar; barn 20x24, 1½ story, well finished; corn crib; two (2) good wells, and other improvements. Price, $20 per acre.

No. 6.—Three and one-half miles from Clay Center; 160 acres very best creek bottom land; 70 acres under cultivation; 25 acres timber; 30 acres pasture fenced; living water; house, stable, etc. Price, $1,600—$800 cash, balance 4 years time.

No. 7.—Six miles from Clay Center 160 acres "A No. 1" land, 60 acres under cultivation; house 14x16; good cellar, stable, granary, cribs, etc.; good well; grove of 1000 maples; 300 fruit trees; a splendid stone quarry ½ mile from farm to go with it. $12.50 per acre; half cash, balance in one year. This is is a handsome farm.

No. 8.—160 acres; 90 under cultivation; 25 acres in timber; living water; house 16x24 with addition 12x16; cellar, good well, stable, grain cribs, etc., etc.; 100 fruit trees; all very best creek bottom land. Price $11 per acre.

No. 9.—80 acres of excellent second bottom land four miles from Morgantown, with 20 acres under cultivation, for $6 per acre.

No. 10.—160 acres of nice rolling land, with a good house and 40 acres broken; 12 miles from Clay Center; with a good team of horses and 6 head of cattle, all for $1,000 cash. This is a bargain.

No. 11.—160 acres of choice land 6 miles from Wakefield, with 80 acres under cultivation, good house, stable, &c., for $10 per acre; 25 acres of fall wheat on the ground thrown in. This is a beautiful farm and a bargain.

No. 12.—160 acres of upland, with 100 acres in good tilth; good house and stone stable; good well and 55 acres of fall wheat on the place, all for $1,500, and only 6 miles from Wakefield; time given on part. We think the wheat on this place will nearly pay for it the coming season.

No. 13.—160 acres of choice creek and river bottom land, with 115 acres under cultivation; good house, stables, crib, and good well, for $3,000; time on part.

No. 14.—160 acres of good bottom land; 25 acres of timber; 40 acres under cultivation; a good well and a good house; 9 miles from Clay Center. Price only $1,300, and four years time given on the most of it.

No. 15.—Eighty acres of excellent land; house 16x18; 40 acres under cultivation; good well and a bargain at $8 per acre. Twelve miles from Clay Center.

No. 16.—160 acres 3 miles from Clay Center with a good house; good well.

No. 17.—200 acres one mile from Clay Center; 120 acres bottom land, 90 acres under cultivation; good house and good well of water; fine orchard of peach trees. $2 per acre.

No. 18.—160 acres 10 miles from Clay Center; 40 acres under cultivation; price $800; two years time on one-half of it; fine rolling land, and worth twice the money.

No. 19—160 acres 2½ miles from Clay Center; 50 acres broke; good house and good well and other improvements. Price $800. This will soon be sold.

No. 20.—¾ of a mile from Clifton 160 acres; 100 acres broken; house 14x24; kitchen 12x14; good well; pasture fenced; wood and water on the place; land lays fine. This is an excellent farm; only $10 per acre.

No. 21.—240 acres 1 mile from Clifton; 110 acres broke; 2½ miles hedge fence that will turn stock in one year; wood and water. This is a very choice farm in every respect. Will sell for $2000; time on part.

No. 22.—160 acres 4 miles from Clifton with 80 acres under cultivation; 2 miles of hedge that will soon turn stock; good well; in every respect a first-class farm now offering for only $12. Time on part.

No. 23.—One mile from Clay Center, 40 acres; 16 broke; good hedge on three sides; fine land. Price, $600. This is a beautiful piece of land and worth twice the money.

No. 24.—Splendid farm of 320 acres 3 miles from Clifton; 150 acres broke; good new frame house, 2 rooms and kitchen all plastered; good well with pump; plenty wood and water. Price $2,000. This is one of the finest farms in this section and a big drive at the price.

No. 25.—136 acres river bottom, 2½ miles from Clay Center; 10 acres broken, house 12x16, good well and living water. Will make a splendid farm. Can be had cheap for cash.

No. 26.—160 acres, 2 miles from Clifton; 12 acres broken, stone house 12x14, good springs. Splendid stock farm.

No. 27.—160 acres of fine farming land, 15 miles from Clay Center, with a 2 story stone house 16x23, well finished; 2 unfailing wells and running water on the place; sheds and stables; plenty of the best building stone; 70 acres bottom land; 3,000 forest trees, 100 fruit trees; school house ½ mile from the house. All offered for $1,500 and time given on $1,000 of that. Buy it.

No. 28.—80 acres 4 miles from Clay Center; 35 broke; house 12 by 14; 12 acres in wheat to go in; 400 forest trees; 25 fruit trees. All for $800, 5 years given on part.

No. 29.—160 acres 7 miles from Clay Center; 40 acres broke; fine rolling land and a beautiful location; stone house, unfinished; well of good water; peach orchard bearing and shade trees in abundance. Price, only $1,200, $700 down and balance on 4 years' time.

REFERENCES.

Anticipating that some may have their doubts, as all Eastern men are apt to, in regard to our country, I take pleasure in referring, *by permission*, to some of our most trustworthy and estimable men and citizens, whom you may address in reference to our country and its advantages, who I am sure will not only corroborate what I have written, but tell you *the half is not here told*.

Farmers' and Merchants' Bank, Clay Center, Kansas.

John Higanbotham, grain and stock dealer, proprietor of the Higanbotham Elevator, Clay Center, Kansas.

C. M. Kellogg, attorney and State Senator for Thirty-second district, Clay Center, Kansas.

Dr. Blackwood, physician and surgeon, Clay Center, Kansas.

John A. Moss, cashier of Farmers' and Merchants' Bank, Clay Center. Kansas.

C. R. Barnes, proprietor of the Quaker City Mills, Clay Center, Kansas.

Harry Higanbotham, cashier Clay County Bank, Clay Center, Kansas.

H. M. Frazer, register of deeds, Clay Center, Kansas.

Clay County Bank, Clay Center, Kansas.

J. P. Campbell, editor Clay County Dispatch, Clay Center, Kan.

TABLE

Showing amount of Grain and other Produce forwarded from Clay Center during 1876.

MONTHS.	Corn, lbs.	Wheat, lbs.	Rye, lbs.	Oats, lbs.	Barley, lbs.	Castor Beans, lbs.	Broom Corn, lbs.	Cattle, head.	Live Hogs, head.	Dressed Hogs, lbs.	Butter, lbs.	Eggs, dozen.
January....	1,667,700	442,250	260,000	20,000	.....	40,000	520	66	245	46,508	7,770	5,340
February ...	2,625,500	600,500	360,400	20,000	.....	20,000	20,000	111	588	14,870	5,250	7,230
March.......	461,600	383,900	140,000	20,000	.....	.....	.....	26	553	.....	1,350	5,220
April.......	995,750	170,000	60,000	40,000	.....	.....	.....	119	344	.....	4,449	6,510
May.........	1,500,000	610,000	120,000	20,000	20,000	.....	.....	111	56	.....	7,405	3,060
June........	2,508,000	530,000	240,000	.....	.....	20,000	20,000	19	48	.....	16,827	1,140
July........	1,466,000	360,000	120,000	.....	.....	.....	.....	142	.....	.....	6,491	630
August......	1,254,000	630,000	694,400	.....	.....	.....	80,000	.....	50	.....	2,655	660
September...	587,300	3,444,000	1,586,800	.....	201,000	.....	80,000	139	89	.....	3,362	2,670
October.....	788,800	3,072,000	1,340,800	.....	1,125,800	.....	160,000	120	139	.....	3,480	1,710
November....	1,345,600	3,432,000	1,089,500	.....	288,800	24,000	80,000	132	550	.....	3,200	990
December....	2,374,400	2,016,000	1,508,000	.....	108,000	.....	80,000	68	1,068	52,000	6,838	1,710
Total.......	17,574,650	15,692,650	7,589,750	120,000	1,843,400	84,000	440,520	1,034	3,730	113,438	69,077	37,470

—*Clay County Dispatch.*

PACIFIC HOTEL.

LOWEST RATES.

Best Accommodations.

THE PATRONAGE OF THE GENERAL TRAVELING PUBLIC SOLICITED.

Through an extended experience in the hotel business we think we have learned how to meet the wants of our guests, and shall use our best efforts to please. When you stop at

JUNCTION CITY

ASK FOR THE

PACIFIC HOTEL,

B. GEMENY, Proprietor.

www.ingramcontent.com/pod-product-compliance
Lightning Source LLC
Chambersburg PA
CBHW030916260626
47169CB00008B/2872